For Amanda, Hannah,
Dylan, Ceri and Kate
J.S.

First published in Great Britain 1995
by William Heinemann Limited
an imprint of Reed Consumer Books Limited
Michelin House, 81 Fulham Road, London SW3 6RB
and Auckland, Melbourne, Singapore and Toronto

0 434 97181 2

Produced by Mandarin Offset Limited
Printed and bound in China

horrible crocodile

Jonathan Shipton

Illustrated by Claudio Muñoz

HEINEMANN · LONDON

This is me
and Mum
and Monkey
going to school.

This is Miss.

This is where I sit.

And this is Steven!

We like our new school.
And we like Miss.
But what we can't stand,
what spoils everything,
is . . .

FLORA!

Because Flora bites!
Because she's a Horrible Crocodile
and she follows us everywhere!
All the time!
Even if we hide.

Even if we say,

"Go away, FLORA!
We don't like
Horrible Crocodiles!"

She gets us in the end.
She creeps up from behind
and she

SNAPS!

And Miss says we can't snap back because
biting is wrong for everyone.
(Even Steven.)

But Flora doesn't care
because she's a crocodile
and crocodiles

DON'T CARE!

One day

the Horrible Crocodile

makes a Horrible Crocodile mistake . . .

She makes Monkey

scREAM

at the top of his voice!
It is so loud
that Flora jumps
right out of her crocodile skin!

And all the playdough turns to rock . . .
And all the babies jump up in their prams.
And the traffic skids to a stop . . .
And the little old ladies drop their bags . . .

And Flora decides
she doesn't want to be a crocodile
any more.

And she is very, very sorry
about Monkey's arm.

So we make him
a hospital bed.

And now he's feeling better.

And so is Flora.

And she's never going to bite anybody . . .

. . . ever again!